Maya Papaya

AND HER AMIGOS

PLAY DRESS-UP

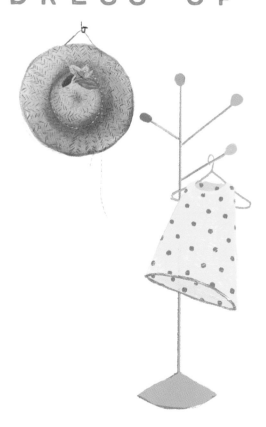

maya
Papaya

AND HER AMIGOS
PLAY DRESS-UP

Susan Middleton Elya • Illustrated by Maria Mola

Charlesbridge

For Kimmy and Kelly—S. M. E.
For Aina, my sweet rainbow lovey—M. M.

Text copyright © 2018 by Susan Middleton Elya
Illustrations copyright © 2018 by Maria Mola

Published by Charlesbridge
85 Main Street
Watertown, MA 02472
(617) 926-0329
www.charlesbridge.com

Library of Congress Cataloging-in-Publication Data
Names: Elya, Susan Middleton, 1955–, author. | Mola, Maria, illustrator.
Title: Maya Papaya and her amigos play dress-up / Susan Middleton Elya; illustrated by Maria Mola.
Description: Watertown, MA: Charlesbridge, [2018] | Text primarily in English with Spanish words. |
Summary: Maya Papaya plays dress-up with her pets and toys every season.
Identifiers: LCCN 2017033094 (print) | LCCN 2017048207 (ebook) | ISBN 9781632896520 (ebook) |
ISBN 9781632896537 (ebook pdf) | ISBN 9781580898034 (reinforced for library use)
Subjects: LCSH: Clothing and dress—Juvenile fiction. | Seasons—Juvenile fiction. |
Play—Juvenile fiction. | Stories in rhyme. | CYAC: Stories in rhyme. | Clothing and dress—
Fiction. | Seasons—Fiction.| Play—Fiction.
Classification: LCC PZ8.3.E514 (ebook) | LCC PZ8.3.E514 May 2018 (print) | DDC [E]—dc23
LC record available at https://lccn.loc.gov/2017033094

Printed in China
(hc) 10 9 8 7 6 5 4 3 2 1

Illustrations done digitally, using a tablet and created with spontaneity and a love for imagining
each character's story.
Display type set in Changing by PintassilgoPrints and Meltow Sans Rust by Typesketchbook
Text type set in Helenita Book
Color separations by Colourscan Print Co Pte Ltd, Singapore
Printed by 1010 Printing International Limited in Huizhou, Guangdong, China
Production supervision by Brian G. Walker
Designed by Susan Mallory Sherman

Maya Papaya has many reasons
to dress up her pets and toys for the seasons.
A hat or a scarf, some gloves or *zapatos*—
she dresses her dog, her stufties, her *gatos*.

LA PRIMAVERA

Winter has passed. See buds on the trees.
Daffodils blooming. More *flores*, please!

Maya Papaya puts on twelve hats—
lovely *sombreros* and caps for her cats.
Feathery, flouncy, flowery, funky—
grab an umbrella and rain boots for monkey.

Maya Papaya puts on *tacones*
to dance with her *tigres* and bears and *leones*.
All her *peluches* silently clap,
while two little *gatos* secretly nap.

EL VERANO

El cielo is blue, the spring rains are over.
Time to go barefoot outside in the clover.

Maya Papaya, in *gafas de sol*,
shares with her friends her pink *parasol*.
In her *traje de baño*, she jumps in the pool,
then lines up the chairs for her pet summer school.

Maya Papaya puts on her wings,
waves her *varita*, and wishes for things.
"*¡Ay, guacamole!* We need lemonade."
Twelve tiny glasses appear in the shade.

EL OTOÑO

The moon is aglow. *El aire* is chilly.
Pumpkins wear faces, scary or silly

Maya Papaya pours everyone tea—
her *gatos*, *perritos*, and *ositos* three!
They sit on *las sillas*, drink from their *tazas*,
and nibble the pie made from orange *calabazas*.

Maya Papaya has three long *rebozos*—
plenty for wrapping up all her stuffed *osos*.
They're at *la ventana*, in a row that is neat,
watching while Maya and kids trick-or-treat.

EL INVIERNO

The air has a bite. *La nieve* has fallen.
Look at it sparkle. The holidays are callin'.

Maya Papaya dons her *capucha*.
Shhh! She calls out to her bestie, "*¡Escucha!*"
The quiet snow dresses up trees *elegantes*,
while she snuggles her bunny and puts on his *guantes*.

Maya shows off her *bufanda* so long,
and grabs the gold mic to sing out a song.
She sings about sledding and riding on *burros*,
snowball fights, *fiestas*, and cocoa with *churros*.

Maya Papaya loves every season.
She dresses so silly without any reason.
In raincoats or swimsuits or woolly *abrigos*,
she sticks with her friends—her furry *amigos*.

GLOSSARY

(los) *abrigos:* (ah BREE goce) coats

(el) *aire:* (I reh) air

(los) *amigos:* (ah MEE goce) friends

    ay, guacamole: (I, gwah kah MOE leh) oh, holy moly

(la) *bufanda:* (boo FAHN dah) scarf

(los) *burros:* (BOO rroce) donkeys

(las) *calabazas:* (kah lah BAH sahs) pumpkins

(la) *capucha:* (kah POO chah) hood

(los) *churros:* (CHOO rroce) sugared donut sticks

(el) *cielo:* (SYEH loe) sky

    elegantes: (eh leh GAHN tehs) elegant

    escucha: (ehs KOO chah) listen

(las) *flores:* (FLOE rehs) flowers

(las) *fiestas:* (FYEHS tahs) parties

(las) *gafas de sol:* (GAH fahs DEH SOLE) sunglasses

(los) *gatos:* (GAH toce) cats

(los) *guantes:* (GWAHN tehs) gloves

(el) *invierno:* (een VYEHR noe) winter

(los) *leones:* (leh OE nehs) lions

(la) *nieve:* (NYEH–veh) snow

(los) *ositos:* (OE SEE toce) teddy bears

(los) *osos:* (OE soce) bears

(el) *otoño:* (oe TOE nyoe) autumn

(el) *parasol:* (pah rah SOLE) sun umbrella

(los) *peluches:* (peh LOO chehs) stuffed animals

(los) *perritos:* (peh RREE toce) puppies

(la) *primavera:* (pree mah VEH rah) spring

(los) *rebozos:* (rreh BOE soce) shawls

(las) *sillas:* (SEE yahs) chairs

(el) *sombrero:* (sohm BREH roe) big hat

(los) *tacones:* (tah KOE nehs) high heels

(las) *tazas:* (TAH sahs) cups

(los) *tigres:* (TEE grehs) tigers

(el) *traje de baño:* (TRAH heh DEH BAH nyoe) swimsuit

(la) *varita:* (vah REE tah) wand

(la) *ventana:* (vehn TAH nah) window

(el) *verano:* (veh RAH noe) summer

(los) *zapatos:* (sah PAH toce) shoes

* *El*, *la*, *los*, and *las* in Spanish mean "the" in English.